EVERYWHERE WITH
WIZZY
HAPPY READING
Anthony Ridgway

WIZZY
and the Seaside Adventure
by Anthony Ridgway
illustrated by Suzan Houching

to Mia and Jessica, with love
Ant and Suzan Houching

Editing and layout by Jenny Knowles

First published in July 2018
Publisher - Little Knoll Press

ISBN No. 978-0-9935078-7-8

Printed in Great Britain by
Biddles Books Limited
Castle House, East Winch Road
Blackborough End, King's Lynn
Norfolk PE32 1SF

'Adventures always come to the adventurous'
Five Go to Smuggler's Top
by Enid Blyton.

My name is Anthony Ridgway. I have cerebral palsy.

I first had the idea for Wizzy because children often stop me when I am out in the local park in my electric wheelchair. They ask their parents, "What is the matter with that man?"

Some people get embarrassed and walk away; sometimes I have to explain, "My legs don't work."

The name Wizzy came about from a friend, Leo, who used to call my chair 'Wizzy Wheelchair'.

Wizzy is a talking wheelchair with attitude! Dan and Wizzy are like two friends. Dan's father designed the chair so that Dan is able to be independent, using Wizzy's amazing abilities. They have some terrific adventures together. I hope you will enjoy reading about them.

My mum and dad, Grethe and Mike, have helped me hugely over the years. My dad used to write things down for me. Sadly, he has now died.

I now write using a computer programme developed by Dolphin Computer Access. I type using a large keyboard and the computer speaks out each letter. In this way I build the sentences. My mum helps me edit, which is especially useful when the programme uses automatic spell check with sometimes amusing results.

I would like to thank my creative writing teacher, Barbara Large, for her support and encouragement since we first met in 2008, and for helping me to polish up my writing.

My first book, *Wizzy the Animal Whisperer,* was launched in 2016 at The Point, Eastleigh. Over 100 people came, including the actor, David Suchet, and his wife, Sheila. An audio version of *Wizzy the Animal Whisperer* was recorded by David and Sheila Suchet, who did all the different voices of the characters between them.

I would like to say thanks to everybody who made my first book possible and for giving Wizzy another adventure, this time at the seaside. Wizzy is brought even more to life by Suzan Houching's wonderful drawings. I am transported down to the seaside every time I look at them.

Thank you from me … and not forgetting Wizzy of course!

THE INSPIRATION FOR THIS STORY

Wizzy and the Seaside Adventure was inspired by my experiences of three places.

First, as a young boy, Mum and Dad, Grethe and Mike, took me several times on holiday to Cornwall. The seaside town for the story in this book is a mixture of Crackington Haven, Padstow and Boscastle.

I remember on one of our holidays, on a wet and misty afternoon, seeing a yellow helicopter hovering over the sea. Below, the coastguard's boat appeared to be searching. We never did find out what for.

The second inspiration comes from Portsmouth, Hampshire, where I used to go wheelchair dancing in the church hall at St Peter and St Paul Church. Across the road from the church is Wymering Manor, which is reputed to be haunted. I was fascinated by its history and its links to the church.

The third place was Pendine Sands in Wales. When Mum and I went to visit John and Pauline Barker, they took us down onto the sand and John wrote the word 'WIZZY' in the sand for me.

Anthony Ridgway

FOREWORD

As Anthony Ridgway's Creative Writing tutor, it is an honour to congratulate him on the publication of his second book, *Wizzy and the Seaside Adventure*.

This beautifully illustrated book is another triumph for Anthony and a testimony to his tenacity, determination and story-telling skills. In wonderful watercolours Suzan Houching truly captures the characters and their escapades, this time by the sea.

Children will love the collaboration between Dan, the boy, and Wizzy, his irascible, cheeky, hi-tech wheelchair. Together they make an excellent team as they join in another scary adventure with friends, James and Sophie, and their dog, Honey.

Readers will soon realise that being in a wheelchair does not prevent Dan, the viewpoint character, from having daring adventures with his able-bodied friends.

Read on, as they chase thieves into a network of mysterious tunnels and end up having to call out the emergency services to rescue both themselves and the thieves.

What will their parents have to say?

Readers, be prepared to be surprised.

Barbara Large MBE
Senior Lecturer Creative Writing
Honorary Fellow University of Winchester
Chairman, Hampshire Writers' Society

Hello, I'm Dan.

I'm sitting in my hi-tech wheelchair. I call him Wizzy, because he really can whiz in all directions at an amazing speed.

My dad designed him especially for me. He has his own number plate on the back, 'WIZZY'. He doesn't need a licence for this.

I can't walk, my legs don't work. My hands do, and my head does too. I can travel anywhere in Wizzy. He's my legs. I simply press an icon on his control box. I steer him with a joystick which has a yellow golf ball on the end of it. It takes him a couple of seconds to stop. I can also use my voice to direct Wizzy.

Inside the control box is a screen, like a smart phone. I can slide it in and out with the press of an icon showing a microphone. This is the special part of Wizzy.

He speaks to me. His voice sounds like the one on your mobile phone when you ask for directions or for a website. He can take photos, record videos and sounds, search the internet, make phone calls, find places, make holograms, hover up and down, make us invisible. He even knows if I am sick.

He's my best friend. He looks after me, keeps me safe. Although he can be very cheeky, Mum trusts him to take me to school, shopping, to the park, even to parties.

WIZZY
and the Seaside Adventure

Wizzy and the Seaside Adventure

"Wow, Wizzy! These cobbled streets are bumpy."

"Affirmative. Dan. They are not doing much for my suspension."

"Hey Wizzy! Look at the buildings overlooking the harbour. They've got crooked roofs and tiny little windows. Do you think they were originally fishermen's houses?

"I love the quaint names of the fishing boats. Look at that blue one. What would give someone the idea to call their boat 'Ollie's Odyssey'?"

"It's a mystery. I have great difficulty understanding human brains. They are illogical."

"Oh, that delicious smell … Cornish pasties! Maybe we'll stop and buy one?"

"I can't smell. Dan … Have no nose. What would your mother say.? You're supposed to be on a diet."

"Oh come on, Wizzy, it's the first day of our holiday in Haven. Who are you anyway, my keeper?"

"Negative. That's no way to speak to me. your best friend."

"Whatever!

Hey, look at that old man over there. He's flapping his arms trying to stop the seagulls from stealing his chips."

"Those pesky gulls better not mess on me.
Eek! Too late, all over my new seat cover."

"Who's the fussy one?"

"Negative. Your mother will not be happy about the extra washing, Dan."

"Since when have you been worried about my mother? She doesn't like you much anyway. Are you planning to get into her good books?"

"I don't know what you mean, Dan.
Is your mother an author?
Is she going to put us in a book?
That would be excellent.
I'll be famous."

"Big head. No, but someone might, one day. It's a saying. OK, as you are so worried about your upholstery, we'll go up the hill. We should be able to see for miles."

"Affirmative. It is six kilometres across the water to the nearest land.
The weather conditions are fair."

"You are so pompous …"

"Oh, good, James and Sophie! What have you been doing and who is this?" I grinned as brother and sister, my two best friends, strolled towards us with a yellow Labrador.

"Nothing much," James replied. "This is Honey, our Nan's dog. We're looking after her while Nan's visiting her cousin in Australia. You? Have you been down to the sea yet?"

"No, we're going up the hill. Wizzy's moaning about seagulls messing on his cover."

"Typical," James laughed. "We'll come with you, Dan."

Sophie pouted. "We were going to explore the rock pools on the beach."

"We can all do that later," James responded.

Sophie glared at him. "You never listen to me. I hate you."

"Dislike, detest, revulsion. I thought you were supposed to love your family members."

"Don't be silly, stupid computer," Sophie shouted.

4

"Negative. Am not stupid. I am extremely clever. You are only a simple child."

"Dan, shut Wizzy up. He's doing my head in." Sophie stamped her feet.

"What's wrong with your head? Is it damaged?"

Sophie's face was a picture. Her cheeks were red, blue eyes flashing, her long fair hair tossing from side to side. I wanted to laugh, but thought better of it … didn't want to make the situation worse.

Instead, I said, "You ought to know Wizzy by now. He takes everything we say literally. Don't let him get to you."

"Negative, am nowhere near her."

"Enough," James broke in, "Let's get on. It's very busy here today, people everywhere."

"You had better watch out for thieves. They go around in gangs of two or three. One will bump into you while the others steal from your pockets."

James smiled. "That wouldn't happen with you around, Wizzy. You'd soon put a stop to them."

"Affirmative."

"Changing the subject," James said, "Let's go and get some fish and chips. I'm starving."

"Negative. You are not short of food. Children in parts of Africa would be grateful for any food. They are starving."

James sighed. "Wizzy sounds like my Nan the way he's going on."

I said, "There's a van over there in the car park. If you and Sophie get the fish and chips, we'll wait for you here."

"Dan, can you hold Honey?" James handed me Honey's lead.

"No one asked me to look after this animal. Nobody ever listens to my opinion."

"I think," James chuckled. "Wizzy's jealous."

"Negative. Am not."

"We'll do it together, OK?" I said.

"Affirmative."

Turning to my friends, I said, "It might be worth a look around that church afterwards."

"It was built 900 years ago. Since then it has undergone several renovations. It belonged to . . . "

"Oh, shut up, Wizzy." James frowned.

"Come on Sophie."

Sophie shivered. "I don't like the look of that house opposite the church. It looks scary. The windows are like black eyes. We won't go there, will we?"

"Haven Manor is a Grade 11 listed building. Its history has been traced back to William the Conqueror. It has a reputation for being haunted by whispering children, furniture being thrown into the air. It was thought to be used by smugglers."

"I'm definitely not going in there," Sophie stated.

James started walking towards the fish and chip van. Sophie skipped after her brother, giving a little wave to me and Wizzy.

I looked across the bay. The sea was like sparkling sapphires, the sand, buttery gold. "It would be lovely to dip my toes in the sea," I thought aloud.

"Negative. Not with me, you're not. The combination of salt water and sand will make my frame rusty. Not to mention what it would do to my circuits."

"Just day dreaming. I wouldn't do anything to cause you any damage, Wizzy. Don't fuss."

"Negative. If you don't mean it, don't say it."

"OK, enough said. Here come James and Sophie. Hey Honey, don't pull my arm off."

Honey strained on her lead, head up, sniffing.

James handed me my food wrapped in white paper. "We bought you cod and chips, Dan. Is that alright?"

Sophie announced, "I've got sausages with plenty of tomato sauce."

"What've you got, James?" I asked.

"Same as you, mate, plus some bottles of water to drink."

"Thanks, pal," I smiled.

"Don't forget me. I helped,' Sophie said.

I grinned. 'Thanks to both of you.'

We had just started eating when a scruffy little dog came up to us. It sniffed our food and Wizzy's wheels Then, very slowly, it lifted a leg and a stream of steaming yellow liquid cascaded out.

"Yeuch!" Wizzy was indignant.

Honey sniffed Wizzy's wheel with interest.

"Stop that sniffing now!" he commanded.

"See what that dog's done to me. Now they'll all be wanting to smell me. I've become a wheeling messenger."

I laughed. "Don't make such a fuss. We can wash it off later."

"Hm, hm, hm . . ." Wizzy grumbled.

We settled down in the warm sunshine, me in Wizzy, James and Sophie sitting on a bench, Honey playing on the grass.

We had just finished eating when we heard shouting.

"Help!" A woman's voice rang out. "A man's just bumped into me. Now my handbag's missing."

We went over to her.

"Did you see what he looked like?" I asked.

"No. It all happened so fast. This girl came up to me to ask for directions. She had a map. We were looking at it. Then I felt a bump. Turned round. Next, they were both gone and so was my handbag."

The woman wrung her hands.

"Exactly what I warned about earlier."

She looked startled as Wizzy spoke. "Who said that?"

I answered, "My wheelchair. He's special."

"Affirmative. I am brilliant."

"How does that help?" the woman sobbed. "It's not going to recover my bag. I had all my holiday money in it. Over £200, it was. What am I going to do?"

She turned away from us as a small crowd gathered around her.

"Call the police," a man in shorts and a sleeveless vest suggested.

"Probably too late," said another.

I whispered to James, "Wouldn't it be great if we could find the culprits?"

"How do you propose we do that?" he responded.

"Wizzy might have camera footage," I suggested. "Have you?" I asked.

"I will review. Give me 20 seconds."

Red lights blinked rapidly on his display screen. "Affirmative! Not clear images. A woman and a man running in the direction of the church. They are looking over their shoulders."

"Let's see," I peered at Wizzy's screen.

James confirmed. "He's right, but the pictures are grainy. Can we zoom in?"

"Was not expecting to produce excellent photographs. Am not a detective."

Sophie frowned. "Does it matter? After all, we only need to have some idea of what they look like and where they went."

"Sophie is a most discerning young person. She is quite right."

Sophie beamed. "You are alright, Wizzy. I like you now."

"Thank you. As a human being you are acceptable too."

I felt impatient. "When you two have quite finished having a mutual appreciation society, we need to get on."

"Now, where were we?" I wondered.

"We were looking at Wizzy's camera footage," said James. "They'll be long gone by now, thanks to Sophie and Wizzy admiring each other."

Exasperated, I said, "Can we please get on with it. We're wasting time. The church is that way." I pointed right. "Hurry up, there's no time to lose."

James and Sophie broke into a run, dragging Honey with them.

"Fast speed, Wizzy."

"Affirmative."

"Slow down." I shouted as we narrowly missed an elderly couple. They clutched each other as we zoomed past.

"Make up your mind."

Wizzy rolled very slowly forward. I sighed. "Just catch up with James and Sophie."

"Affirmative."

Arriving at the church, Wizzy and I wheeled in.

Peering into the gloom, I called, "James, Sophie. Where are you?"

Honey ran up to us, her tail wagging.

Sophie popped out from behind a stone pillar. The sun's rays shining through the stained glass window sparkled around her hair like a halo.

"What took you so long?" she called out.

"Hm, hm, hm . . ." Wizzy grumbled.

"What's the matter?" she asked.

"Forget it," I said. "Some wheelchairs have no common sense."

"Negative. I am very clever."

"Now look what you've started. Where's James?"

"Over there." Sophie pointed towards the altar. "It's weird. They've disappeared."

"There you are." James came up to us, brushing cobwebs from his hair. "I thought you'd got lost."

"Negative. My directional abilities are never impaired."

"Here we go again. Wizzy, he didn't really believe we were lost."

"Why did he say it then?"

"It's just another expression. Forget it."

"Affirmative. Deleting from my memory.'"

Sophie giggled.

I scowled at her. "Don't say anything, please. Otherwise we'll never get on."

She turned away, hand over her mouth.

"I don't understand." James looked perplexed. "We've looked everywhere. No sign of them."

"Vanished," agreed Sophie.

I had an idea. "Wizzy, old churches often have priest tunnels, don't they?"

"Affirmative. There is one in the vestry. It goes directly to the Manor House."

"Oh, no," wailed Sophie. "Not going there." She sat down with a thump.

"You stay here then," I reassured.

"I'm not staying here on my own," Sophie said. "What if they come back?"

"No, you are not," James stated. "If anything happens to you, I'll be in big trouble. Anyway you're too young to be left by yourself."

"Am not. I'm nearly eight. Anyway, Honey can stay with me."

"Where is she? That's all we need. Where is that dog?" James looked stern, arms across his chest. "You will come with us and that's the end of it."

"Interesting debate. Unhelpful, unproductive. Shall we proceed?"

Tears ran down Sophie's cheeks.

James put his arm around her. "Come on. We need your sharp eyes."

She sniffed. "OK," she muttered.

"Back to the matter in hand," I reminded them. "How will we find them?"

"I will deploy my heat seeking capabilities."

"Excellent. Great thinking, Wizzy," I said.

"Affirmative. I am good. Starting now."

We waited … then waited some more. Wizzy's screen flashed, red light blinking.

Honey ran up to us, her tail wagging, scampering around us, excited.

Sophie hugged Honey. "Not now, daft dog. We're busy."

"How long is this going to take?" I asked. "They'll be in Scotland at this rate."

"What am I? A miracle worker? Just discounting non-human life forms."

"Do you mean what I think …?" began James.

I shot him a warning look. I didn't want to scare Sophie.

"Oh." He mouthed the word, "r-a-t-s."

"What did you say?" demanded Sophie. "Not ghosts?" She shivered.

"No. Don't worry," James said. "There are none. Just a silly story."

"Detecting human activity in the Manor House."

"Let's go." My voice shook a little. I did feel nervous.

"Are you frightened, Dan?" Sophie asked.

"Wizzy will look after us, won't you?"

"Take care of, guard, mind . . ."

"Yes, yes, you've got it." I held my hand up. "Here we are, in the vestry. We need to be very quiet."

Honey ran up to one of the walls, whining.

Sophie touched her. "What is it girl? What's there?"

"The dog's found the entrance. Powerful sense of smell, typical in dogs. She's not clever enough to tell you how to get in. Not superior like me.

James, put your hand on the cross carved on that panel."

James reached up. As his hand pressed down, the panel slid to his right with a swoosh.

The air smelt cold and damp. I couldn't see anything in the darkness.

14

"How far is it to the Manor House, Wizzy? Can we risk using your lights?"

"They are bright. They would help you to see. They may also alert the thieves. Do you want them or not? I don't need them. My navigation is perfect."

I pulled a face. Wizzy is so conceited, I thought. "No, we'd better not. You two, hold on to Wizzy while he guides us. Keep Honey under control. Don't let her go ahead of us."

We began moving.

Sophie squealed. "I can't keep up. You're going too fast. Ooh. What was that? Something touched my face."

"Probably cobwebs," James answered. "Nothing to worry about. Wizzy, can you go at a slower pace please? We don't have wheels."

"Affirmative. You have two legs, not efficient means of transport."

I broke in. "Just a minute. Where will we come out of the passage?"

"The library. My sensors show two humans near the opening."

"They'll see us, won't they?" James said with a groan.

"Affirmative. You will be visible."

Sophie whimpered. "I'm scared. Let's go back."

"No, we are not. We've come this far. I for one am going to see this through. We must catch them red-handed." I felt determined.

"Negative. No red paint. Illogical. Explain."

I sighed. "It's just an …"

"An expression." Wizzy completed my sentence.

We proceeded slowly. Wizzy's wheels squeaking slightly.

I was wondering how we could avoid a confrontation with the thieves, when James exclaimed, "I've an idea. Wizzy, can you create holograms so that they appear to be coming out of the opening to the passage?"

I said, "Wizzy can do almost anything, except swim. Great thinking, James."

"Affirmative. What do you want me to create?"

"What about children?" I suggested. "Wizzy, didn't you tell us something about children whispering?"

"Not very scary," Sophie responded.

"No, that's right." James agreed. "We need something spectacular to draw attention away from us."

"What then?" I puzzled.

"Pirates," exclaimed Sophie. "That would do it."

"Well done, Sophie. That's a great idea. OK, Wizzy?" I asked.

"Affirmative. Which ones do you want? Factual or fictional?"

"I don't know, fictional, I think. What have you got on your database?" I said.

"Captain Hook from *Peter Pan*.
Long John Silver from *Treasure Island*.
The Black Pirate from *The Black Pirate*."

James looked puzzled. "Never heard of the last one.
Where DO you get it from, Wizzy?"

"My general knowledge is superb . . ."

"OK, OK, no time for explanation. Let's have a mash up
of all those characters, but scary, like the actual pirates
who smuggled here."

"Affirmative. I await your instructions.
I could make sounds too if you wish."

Laughing, I said, "Is there no end to your talents? No, don't need an answer
Come on. Remember we need to be very quiet."

"Yes," agreed James. "We want to give them an element of surprise."

I held up my hand. "What I suggest we do is, when we reach
the entrance to the library, Wizzy creates the pirate
hologram with his lasers. With any luck, they'll
be startled and we can slip in unnoticed."

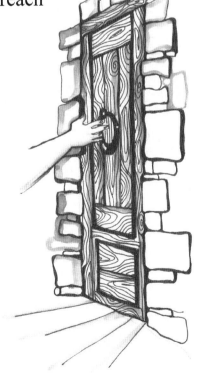

"Affirmative. Thirty seconds.
James, put your hand out. I will deploy
my lights to show you where to pull."

In front of us we saw a wooden panel
with a metal ring.

"Here goes," breathed James. He tugged at the ring.

The panel slid silently to the right and air rushed
into the tunnel, brushing our faces.

"NOW, Wizzy! Do it NOW," I instructed.

In front of us a fearsome pirate appeared. He had long hair, partially covered by a black tri-cornered hat. His long coat, a dark green, a sword hung from his belt. Thigh high, scuffed leather boots completed his outfit.

"What have we here, me hearties?" he intoned in a deep, dark,

resounding voice.

Sophie whispered, "He's really good. Just like the real thing."

She giggled.

Honey gave a short bark.

"Shush," I warned.

Beyond the pirate, I saw two people, a woman and a man, look up from a table near the opening.

On the table were bank notes, coins, watches, mobile phones, cameras, a handbag – a real Aladdin's cave.

The woman, her dark hair pulled back into a pony tail, wearing a grey sweatshirt and jeans, screamed.

Her hands flew to her mouth.

Her companion pulled the top of his hood down off his head, showing his unshaven face.

He growled, "Cindy, shut up. You'll give the game away. I knew you would be trouble, didn't want to bring you on this job in the first place."

Cindy's voice quivered. "They said this place was haunted. We've got to get away from it before it cuts us to ribbons. And the children too … I'm sure I heard whispering, giggling and barking."

"Stupid woman, it's just some trickery to keep people away. Back to business. Ignore it."

"Wizzy," I whispered. "Do something to really frighten them. We've got to get them to move away from the evidence … a loud noise, like an explosion?"

"Affirmative." I read on his screen.

James, Sophie and I waited, hardly daring to breath.

The pirate leapt into action, yelling in a terrifying voice,

"Light the gunpowder. We'll rid us of these low lifes."

This was followed by "BOOM! BOOM! BOOM!"

The floor appeared to tremble.

Honey broke into frenzied barking, straining at her leash.

Cindy shrieked, "I don't care, Pete. I'm off.

Not waiting to be torn to shreds."

Pete pulled his hands through his lank, greasy hair. He too was looking scared now.

"OK, let's go. Not through the front door. That booming may have attracted attention. Can't be seen. Don't want to be caught."

Tears streaming, Cindy snuffled, "We can't go back that way, the pirate's blocking the passage. What are we going to do?"

"Follow me and stop snivelling," Pete shouted.

Sophie giggled.

"What was that?" Cindy peered across the room.

"Never mind," he said, grabbing a handful of the stolen goods.

The pirate shot towards him.

"Stop right there, you scurvy landlubbers."

The two took to their heels,

shot out of the room.

James said, "This way, we'll follow them."

"We should notify someone about what we've found here, first," I said.

"You mean, ring the police?" queried Sophie.

"Negative. No signal. Even I cannot make a call."

We moved into the library.

"Better not touch anything," warned James.

"Why?" Sophie asked.

"Evidence. If your fingerprints are on the stolen goods, you might be accused of being the thieves."

James grinned, "How right you are, oh mighty one."

"Affirmative. I am."

"More to the point, where have they gone?" I reminded the others.

"Down the second passage."

"Why didn't you tell me that there was another one, Wizzy," I exclaimed.

"You only had to ask. I can't read your mind."

"Never mind that now. Where does it go?"

"It's a smuggler's tunnel. They used it to bring in illegal contraband, like money and alcohol, from hijacked ships."

"Wow, that's so exciting! How do we get there?" asked James.

"Negative. Not going there. They are heading towards a cave which is rapidly filling with sea water. It will be high tide in fifteen minutes. I will not be damaged."

"Oh no, we've sent them to their deaths," Sophie gasped.

"Serve them right . . . logical punishment."

James scratched his head. "So, without a signal we can't let the coastguard or the police know."

Sophie shouted. "Yes, we know that … duh!"

I suggested, "What if we go back to where we were earlier? We can phone from there."

James and Sophie looked at each other, nodded in agreement.

23

Five minutes later, we came out of the church. It was as if time had stood still. Holiday makers were milling around, an ice cream van was parked down on the quayside, families were queuing, children squabbling.

My mouth began to water. Perhaps later, I thought.

"999 in progress."

"Police, fire or ambulance?" asked the operator.

I took a deep breath. "Police and coastguard, please. We want to report a theft and the thieves are in danger of being drowned."

I started to explain what had happened.

"What do you mean … secret passages, pirates, ghosts? Don't you know making hoax calls is an offence." She rang off.

"That was hopeless," I said.

"We've wasted five minutes just talking about it," said James. "I've an idea. I noticed a path leading up the cliff."

"How will that help?" Sophie asked.

"Yeah, how?" I echoed.

"If you give me a minute, I'll explain," James replied. "I've a hunch it could lead us above the cave where the two are trapped. Am I right, Wizzy?"

"Affiirmative. You are a most intelligent person."

"I don't understand," I puzzled. "What's the point of going up there?"

"When we get there, Wizzy can call the coastguard. We'll tell them we're in trouble ourselves, and then we can alert them to the two below."

"What a clever brother!" exclaimed Sophie.

"Come on then. Show us the way," I instructed.

James pointed. "We need to go back down through the town, past the gift shops and food outlets and around the harbour."

A few minutes later, we began climbing. The path became narrow and rocky. Wind howled around our ears. Sea spray covered us in a fine mist.

"Dan, we should turn back. This is unsafe."

James turned to me. He looked worried. "I'll go on. You and Sophie stay here with the dog."

"No, we're carrying on. We're in this together."

"Too right!" Sophie agreed, looking pale.

My heart was in my mouth. Several times, we nearly toppled over as Wizzy's wheels slipped on loose gravel. Thank goodness for his stabilisers!

Our progress was painfully slow. Honey ran ahead, then came back. She seemed to be checking that we were alright.

"How much further?" I asked.

"Two metres."

"Keep going. No time to lose!"

"Negative. This is as far as we can go, Dan."

Wizzy stopped, refusing to move.

"Wizzy, try ringing the coastguard now," commanded James.

"Affirmative. Mayday, Mayday, three children and a wheelchair trapped on a cliff path above Haven."

I checked my watch. We had been on the path for five minutes. "How long will it be before the rescue gets here?"

"Three minutes, twenty seconds."

I felt scared, but I wasn't going to say so. Each gust of wind buffeted Wizzy, causing him to rock in a really scary way.

"Your heart rate is rising, Dan. Are you afraid?"

"No, of course not!"

The minutes dragged by. I was shivering with cold and fear.

Sophie put her arm around me. "Here they are now," she said. "Listen, there's a helicopter. And there's a lifeboat down there."

James peered over the edge of the cliff. "They've spotted our two criminals. They're throwing a lifebelt to them."

"Can I see?" Sophie moved towards her brother.

"Negative. Stay with Dan. Don't want you to slip."

We heard shouting on the path behind us.

"Oh, it's the police," Sophie exclaimed. "We'll be safe now."

"James, could you tell the police what we know. Pete and Cindy probably won't let on about their activities, will they? They'll disappear as soon as they can."

Two puffing policeman came up to us.

"How did you lot get up here?" one of them said. "Let's get you to safety … then you've got some explaining to do.
You, in the wheelchair, what's your name?"

"Dan, and these are my friends, James and Sophie. My wheelchair's called Wizzy. Oh, and this is Honey." I pointed at the dog.

"OK, Dan. Can you reverse very slowly?"

"Back up, Wizzy," I instructed.

We started to move. Wizzy's wheels began to slip. Honey whined.

"If we move another centimetre, we will be off the path and onto the rocks below."

"Amazing, Tom," the first policeman exclaimed, "a talking wheelchair!"

"Affirmative. I have many abilities. I require your assistance to ensure my stability."

Tom laughed. "We've seen some strange sights, Brad, but never anything like this."

Brad whistled, said to me, "Full of itself, your chair."

"Negative. Illogical. If I were. I would not exist."

Tom interrupted. "Argumentative too!
Right, I'll go in front of Dan.
You go behind, Brad."

"Negative. Only stating facts.
Be careful. My systems are sensitive."

We made our way back to the
harbour, James and Sophie scrambling in front,
Tom and Brad holding onto Wizzy, Honey following behind.

Down on the quayside, Tom and Brad listened to James.
It seemed as if their eyes were popping out of their heads.

Moving away, Tom spoke into his radio.

I couldn't catch what he was saying, but I had
a pretty good idea that it wouldn't be long before
Pete and Cindy were arrested.

Tom came back to us.
"You children have helped us
more than you know.
We've been after these
two crooks for weeks now.
Pete, in particular, is the
leader of the gang.
Well done!"

"What about me? I am not a child.
I am an extraordinary machine.
I was most instrumental in assisting
in the discovery of the criminals."

Together, James, Sophie and I burst into laughter.

Honey barked, jumping up at us.

Between chuckles, I said, "That's right.
You are not just any wheelchair,
you are my Wizzy
and we couldn't have done it without you."

"Affirmative."

31

MORE WIZZY STORIES

Wizzy the Animal Whisperer – the first Wizzy book by Anthony Ridgway and Suzan Houching, available from www.LittleKnollPress.com and from your local bookshop by request.

The audiobook *Wizzy the Animal Whisperer* read in voices by David and Sheila Suchet – a delightful rendering of the story with all its humour, available to buy from www.LittleKnollPress.com or on loan from Calibre Audio Library.

The audiobook *Wizzy's Worm* recorded by the local radio station Mix96 – available on loan from Calibre Audio Library.

You might also like to watch these VIDEOS on YouTube:
Just go to YouTube and search using the titles in italics below:

How I Write by Anthony Ridgway – Anthony demonstrates how he uses a special computer programme to write.

Wizzy and the Seaside Adventure – Anthony and Suzan plan and discuss illustrations for the book.

BBC South news item on the *Wizzy the Animal Whisperer* launch –
https://www.facebook.com/BBCSouthNews/videos/1174651015958820/